Dedicated to being different, and to making
a difference in one's own time

Copyright © 2020 Gregg Robins
Illustrations by Charity Russell

ISBN 978-2-8399-2992-9

All rights reserved. No part of this book may be
reproduced in any form or by any electronic or
mechanical means including information storage
and retrieval systems - unless it was used in brief
quotations in reviews or articles - without the
permission in writing from the author.

SILENZIO,
SOUND THE ALARM!

WRITTEN BY
GREGG ROBINS

ILLUSTRATED BY
CHARITY RUSSELL

This is the story of a gentle little alarm clock named Silenzio. Silenzio was a handsome clock, with a variety of quite pleasant features.

But he had one major flaw. A flaw that would doom any alarm clock, and is avoided at all costs by alarm clock makers everywhere.

Silenzio was created with a conscience. "What is a conscience?" you ask. A conscience is like a little voice in your head that tells you when something is right or wrong. "But that seems like a good thing, so why is it a problem?" you ask. Well, an alarm clock's mission in life is to wake people up, and a conscience is the one thing that can cause an alarm clock to have second thoughts and to feel empathy. "Wait, what is empathy?" you ask, "and what does it have to do with our story?" Empathy means that you understand and care about how other people feel. So, now do you see what the problem is for an alarm clock with a conscience? Just at the moment it is about to pounce, to sound its alarm and wake a person from a deep sleep, it hesitates. An alarm clock with a conscience sees people sleeping and feels sad and guilty about waking them up from their dreams. That is why a conscience is a huge problem for an alarm clock!

You will soon understand what all of this has to do with Silenzio, so don't be alarmed. But first, you need to learn more about Silenzio's story and what makes him tick…

Silenzio was born into a large family of clocks. Though not widely known, clocks have families, and the most successful clock families have been able to withstand the test of time. Silenzio's grandfather clock was the head of the family, and was big and tall. Silenzio really looked up to him. Silenzio's parent clocks were loving and supportive of him and his siblings, but they preferred to stay in the background and let their children clocks shine. Silenzio's brother and sister clocks were all well known. Ringer was the eldest brother clock, with a ring like a giant marching band, and an impressive record of waking up all sorts of people at all hours of the night and day. Close behind was Banger, with a ring like an elephant stampede, though still a bit untested in key moments. Howler was the runt of the family and, though tiny, produced a memorable howl like a pack of wolves. Tickler was the little sister: she was beautiful to see, and had a lovely ring that sounded like birds chirping. But she always needed to ring more loudly to be heard over her brother clocks, and sometimes she struggled to wake people up.

And the life mission of an alarm clock is what? Yes, to wake people up. Very good - you are paying attention.

All the clocks in Silenzio's family were created
in a small town in America called Clockville. His
ancestor clocks had come from Italy to America during
the great clock migration in the early 1900s, and that is where
his Italian name came from. Silenzio was the only one in his
clock family with an Italian name, something he was very proud of.

Clocks in Clockville began their days by going to clock school. Yes, clock school, where clocks perfect their craft on children, which is very important training because children are the most difficult people to wake up! Especially when they need to go to school. I think you know what I mean. Children pretend they cannot get up, and they sometimes pull a pillow or a blanket over their heads to hide. They even do something really insulting to an alarm clock: they turn it off and pretend it never rang. Sometimes, their parents believe the alarm clock is defective, and they even take it back to the store. The truth is that there has never, ever been a defective alarm clock, a secret known by children all over the world. Adults have never figured this out. "Why?" you ask. Because alarm clocks are the only ones that know and they are not able to speak. This is not the only thing that children know and adults have not figured out, of course.

Silenzio did not do well in clock school. Because of his conscience, he was unable to wake up any children. Despite regular meetings with his parent clocks and teacher clocks, and all of their help and support, Silenzio was never able to sound his alarm. You have probably guessed by now that this is how Silenzio got his name - a highly unusual and most unfortunate name for an alarm clock.

TIME TABLES

After years of Silenzio trying and not succeeding to wake anyone up, his parent clocks had to make a painful decision. They decided to send young Silenzio to Switzerland, with its long and rich clock history. Silenzio would surely learn there how to sound his alarm and to fulfill his life's mission. And so, he was sent packing as he waved his long and short hands and said goodbye to his grandfather clock, his parent clocks, and all his brother and sister clocks. What he did not know, and could not possibly know, was that this journey was going to change his life forever...

Silenzio arrived in Switzerland with his parent clocks' highest hopes that he would return someday with a new face. The best clocks in the world are made in Switzerland, even cuckoo clocks. "What are cuckoo clocks?" you ask. They are fancy contraptions with moving parts, hanging chimes, and colorful housings that make all sorts of strange sounds!

Many people like cuckoo clocks, but alarm clocks do not like them at all. Alarm clocks think cuckoo clocks are too fancy.

But more importantly, alarm clocks do not like them because they just hang around looking pretty and making funny noises. They do not wake people up, which is an alarm clock's mission in life!

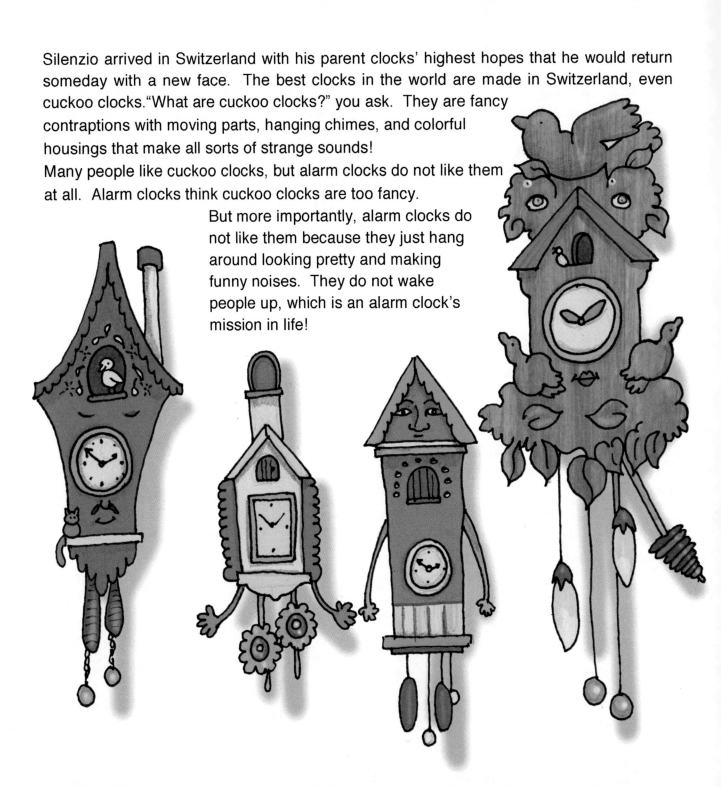

cuckooo! cuckooo!

Silenzio went to a clock boarding school on the shores of Lake Geneva. It was not easy to get into such a school, and Silenzio had no idea how lucky he was just to be there. He was also much closer to Italy, his ancestral home, which was only next door. But still, he missed his home, and he missed grandfather clock, his parent clocks, and Ringer, Banger, Howler and, most of all, little Tickler. Of course, he made new clock friends, but they were not the same for him as his clock family.

The first year in clock school was extremely difficult, and Silenzio was often quite tired. Other clocks noticed Silenzio's problem with his conscience, and they took great pleasure in winding him up over it. Like people, alarm clocks are not always nice to each other, especially when one of them seems different. No matter the efforts of the finest teacher clocks, Silenzio could not ignore his conscience and overcome his inability to sound his alarm. Even the school's clock counsellor was unable to help him. Silenzio seemed destined for an alarm-free life, and the easy life was no life for an alarm clock! But just as he was losing all hope, things started to change.

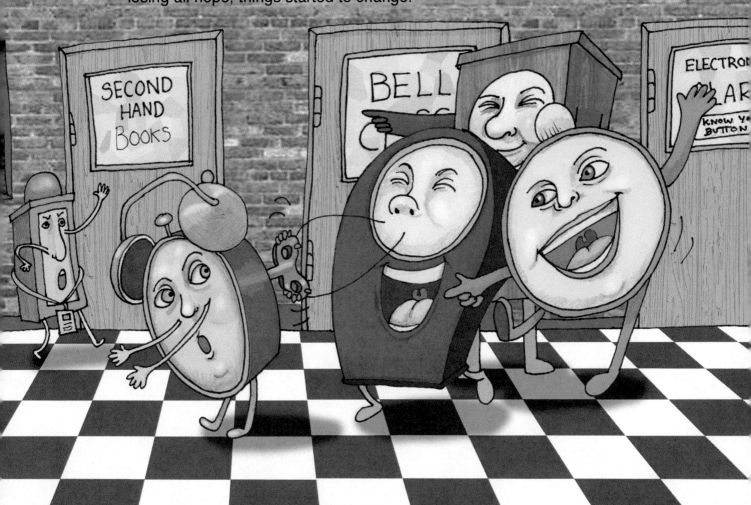

Tired and frustrated, Silenzio was sent to spend the summer vacation with a large Swiss family. He had hoped to go to his home, but needed to spend more time learning to sound his alarm. He was quite sad. But at least he was able to be in a beautiful, tiny Swiss village in the mountains overlooking Lake Geneva.

And it was so quiet, which is always good for alarm clocks, since it make it easier for them to be heard.

In alarm clock folklore, there are tales of alarm clocks in big cities being drowned out by traffic and street noise and feeling quite useless.

"Great, a big family," Silenzio sighed, knowing that children meant trouble, and he might be in for a very long summer indeed. But he took his place with the other alarm clocks and braced himself for whatever the summer might bring. Each morning, the eight children were awoken by their alarm clocks, apart from Lily, the little girl who Silenzio was supposed to awaken, but who he always wanted to leave sleep just a bit longer.

Then one night, something unusual happened...

Silenzio sensed something was wrong. He saw Lily growing uncomfortable in her bed, but did not understand why. She was tossing and turning instead of sleeping soundly, as she always did. He realised that since it was the middle of the night the other alarm clocks would not be paying attention. They were not set to go off for hours! These alarm clocks, you see, slept soundly because they did not have a conscience, and certainly did not possess empathy. They didn't even know what it was! Silenzio watched Lily with increasing concern as she stirred uncomfortably in her bed. "What was wrong?" you ask. Well, as it turns out, unbeknownst to anyone, there was a gas leak in the house, and it was spreading rapidly. The parents were asleep as well, and all the children seemed destined to keep sleeping through it. They could be poisoned, or their house could catch on fire, and they did not even know it. Silenzio did not know there was a gas leak (Come on, you don't think alarm clocks can smell, do you?), but he did know something was wrong from how he observed Lily tossing and turning. He also knew that time was not on his side.

Silenzio could take it no more! With the other alarm clocks paying no attention, he decided to do something he had never been able to do his entire life. Yes, he sounded his alarm. And what an alarm it was! All at once, it rang like a giant marching band, banged like an elephant stampede, howled like a pack of wolves, and tickled like birds chirping. It reached all the children, wherever in the house they were sleeping.

One-by-one they awoke, their parents too, and immediately everyone smelled the gas. Just as time was slipping away, they all ran out of the house and down to the lake. Neighbors gathered on the lawn to watch the spectacle as the gas caused a small fire in the kitchen. With the children looking on as well, fire engines soon arrived. The firemen managed to put out the fire and limit the damage to the home. They even saved all the alarm clocks inside, just in the nick of time, a lucky break for the alarm clocks - they had refused to leave, as they still needed to wait a few more hours to ring.

Silenzio's heroic tale became famous across Switzerland, and in many other countries. He showed the world that having a conscience and feeling empathy were more important than being the best alarm clock in the class, or simply having the loudest ring. He also showed everyone that even the quietest among us can raise our voices the loudest when it is needed most.

With his newfound success and confidence, Silenzio was able to graduate from the Swiss clock school with honours, and was granted his greatest wish: to return home to Clockville to be with his clock family. When he arrived in Clockville, the town was waiting to give him a hero's welcome, with a ticker-tape-tick-tock parade! As he approached Ringer, Banger, Howler, and Tickler, he put his long and short hands together – something clocks do when they are happy – and greeted them with great joy and relief. Silenzio's parent clocks rang out in happiness, and his grandfather clock proudly chimed in his congratulations, in Italian, of course – Bravissimo!

In the end, Silenzio turned out to be a hero. Just when it was most important, he followed his conscience, showed empathy, and sounded "the alarm heard 'round the world." But then again, I guess most of you knew that for Silenzio, it was only a matter of time.

ABOUT THE AUTHOR

Gregg Robins is the proud dad of three millennial daughters. When they were younger, Gregg enjoyed creating stories for them. "Silenzio, Sound the Alarm" is Gregg's first children's book. He once dropped out of high school, later received a PhD from Oxford University, and has always resisted being awoken by alarm clocks of all shapes and sizes. A native New Yorker, Gregg now lives in Geneva, Switzerland, with his wife, and is already planning more adventures for little Silenzio and his alarm clock family!

ABOUT THE ILLUSTRATOR

Charity Russell is a children's book illustrator, her own books include, Mummy's Got MS, Light and The Window Book. Originally from Zambia she moved to the U.K. as a teenager, and now lives in Bristol, England with her husband, two children and their dog Frank.

Charity uses her mobile phone as her alarm, she wishes it was more like Silenzio because she hates getting up in the morning!

www.charityrussell.com

Made in the USA
Middletown, DE
19 November 2020

24493588R00020